Ten Little Bears

A Counting Rhyme

by **Kathleen Hague**

illustrated by **Michael Hague**

SCHOLASTIC INC.

New York Toronto London Auckland Sydney
Mexico City New Delhi Hong Kong

ISBN 0-439-21016-X

Text copyright © 1999 by Kathleen Hague.
Illustrations copyright © 1999 by by Michael Hague.
All rights reserved.
Published by Scholastic Inc., 555 Broadway, New York, NY 10012,
by arrangement with Morrow Junior Books,
a division of William Morrow & Company, Inc.
SCHOLASTIC and associated logos are trademarks and/or
registered trademarks of Scholastic Inc.

12 11 10 9 8 7 6 5 4   5 6 7/0

Printed in the U.S.A.   40

First Scholastic printing, October 2000

Watercolors and pen-and-ink were used for the full-color illustrations.
The text type is 28-point Worcester Round.

For
Jennifer,
Scott,
Mieke,
Patrick,
and
Josef

Love from Michael and Kathleen

10

Little Bears,
Time to rise and shine.
One stayed in bed—
Then there were nine.

9

Little Bears,
Learning how to skate.
One slipped and fell—
Then there were eight.

8

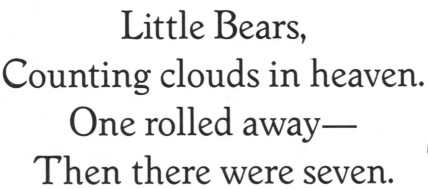

Little Bears,
Counting clouds in heaven.
One rolled away—
Then there were seven.

7

Little Bears,
Built a house of sticks.
One got a splinter—
Then there were six.

6

Little Bears,
Searching for a hive.
One got stung—
Then there were five.

5

Little Bears,
Playing on the shore.
One sailed away—
Then there were four.

4

Little Bears,
Climbing up a tree.
One tumbled down—
Then there were three.

3

Little Bears,
Playing peekaboo.
One got scared—
Then there were two.

2

Little Bears,
Racing in the sun.
One got too hot—
Then there was one.

1

Little Bear,
Tired from all the fun.
Went home to nap—
Then there were none.

No Little Bears—
Is this how our story ends?

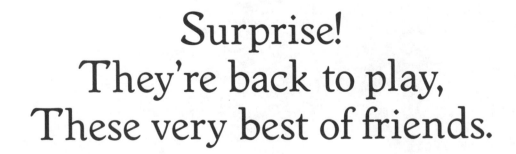

Surprise!
They're back to play,
These very best of friends.